I0547751

Shadow and Light

2017 Savant Poetry Anthology

Edited by Helen R. Davis

Savant Books and Publications
Honolulu, HI, USA
2017

Published in the USA by Savant Books and Publications
2630 Kapiolani Blvd #1601
Honolulu, HI 96826
http://www.savantbooksandpublications.com

Printed in the USA

Edited by Helen R. Davis
Cover Image © Dharshani | Dreamstime.com -
    Solar Eclipse 34926106
Cover Design by Daniel S. Janik

13 digit ISBN: 978-0-9972472-8-2

Table of Contents
(in order of appearance)

Foreward   **1**
Rose Seaquill   **2**
  Grandma In Hawaiian Is Called Tutu
  Peering Into the Looking Glass
  Transgender Niece
Bipul Banerjee   **6**
  Maturity
  Dance in the Rains
Dr. Mike   **10**
  We Can Never Be Happy Again
Doc Krinberg   **14**
  Clarity
  The Girl in Shinjuku Station
  North Shore Return
Jock Armour   **18**
  Ode to the Cereus
Mr. Ben   **24**
  Poured Out Thoughts:My Thoughts
    Heralding God's Magnificence
    Family
    Nature's Blessings
    Save Humanity
    Dad Love Me
Emily Anderson   **32**
  TO C-JAY
Marianne Smith   **36**
  Love Will Find a Way
Carolina Casas   **40**
  Dark Existence
  Imagined Lives
Cigeng Zhang   **46**
  Calla Lily
  The Night of Love
  Who Do I Meet?
  Game

Fish
Thomas Koron   52
  Lament of the Banshee
  Shining Eyes in the Dark
  Fireflies
  On This Bed of Roses
Mark Daniel Seiler   58
  The Bare Tree State
Dwight Armbrust Jr   60
  One Love Can Not Count
  Poison Less Potions
  Candles as Organs
Uhene   64
  O' Be The Light In My Life To Shine Forth...
  O2 Thomas
  So Shook The Earth That Nigh Of Night
  Be Cleansed By A Hand Of Love
  Called to be What I Truly Could and Should Be
Daniel S. Janik   70
  Phantoms of the Night
  New Walls
  Another Poem Echo
  Decidedly Exogenous
Lonner F. Holden   78
  Midspan Hercules
  Wiser Trees
  Mother Moon
  Pointillist
  Opening the Door One Morning
Sara Hawley   86
  I Can't Live Without You
Ihar Kazak   88
  The Ha-Ha Society: A Modern Fable
  Checks and Balances
Barbara Bailey   94
  Ballet of the Undulates
  Would, Could, Should
  Autumn's Song
  Burn Out

V. Bright Saigal   **100**
  Jingles of Laughter
  Percussion of Waves
Ken Rasti   **104**
  Deeper than the Sea
  Sailing
  Sweet Moon
  Nature's Ecstasy
  Dolphins
Teuta S. Rizaj   **112**
  What of Truth?
  But What of Love?
  A Moment of Silence
  The Truest Joy is a Serious Concern
    (Res Severa Verum Gaudium)

Foreword

As the publisher of the Savant Poetry Anthology, I am proud to say that this, our seventh in the series over eight years, is truly exceptional. Not only does it include more poets than ever before (twenty-three to be exact), but it contains more award-winning and multi-award poets.

While we never thematize our anthologies, a theme typically emerges as we pick, choose and order the year's best poems, and this year's emerging theme and its title, SHADOW AND LIGHT, are most appropriate. Not only does this year's anthology plumb the depths of shadow but it equally scales the heights of light, and in the process, presents the reader with not only the extremes, but by their mere presence together in one edition, a singular canvas of the human condition.

But that's not all. This year, perhaps more than any other, our anthology has a decidedly different "feel" to it: one that both indirectly and directly reflects the increasingly unique point-of-view of our newest generation. I could expound on this, but I think it better to simply point it out, and leave it to the reader to discover and enjoy this particularly unique aspect to this year's edition.

Nanea i ka heluhelu iho
(enjoy the read)

- Daniel S. Janik, Publisher

Rose Seaquill is the pen name of Loya Whitmer - it comes from her love the smell of roses, living by the sea, and her use of the poet's pen. Living on Kauai, Rose has been writing poetry since the Eighties. She has been working as an artist since 2008, and is currently embedding artistic works alongside her poems into a book. She is passionate about her three businesses:

AngelsTouchMassageKauai.com

WildHoneyMassage.com

AngelsSandCrafts&Art in Kauaikeepsakes.com

Her published works include GRANDMA'S ART COLORING BOOK.

Helen R. Davis (Ed)

Grandma In Hawaiian Is Called Tutu
to women and balance within

Recognized for her beneficial gifts
Her unique ability to accept major shifts
An elderly woman may be called Tutu Wahine in Hawaiian
Whose wisdom comes of her strife-driven travels into Zion.

THERE WAS A TIME WHEN MISSIONARIES SUP-
PRESSED HAWAIIAN CULTURE

For at least two hundred years
Christain missionaries suppressed Hawaiian culture and belief;
Hawaiian studies are now part of the education curriculum
To the degree that we no longer experience the culture vulture.

WHAT A RELIEF

Tutu Angeline remembers her ancestors.
She memorized them when young,
Chanting her ancestors as treasures.
One in each family is chosen to memorize their

ROOTS

So many believe it's too sacred to desecrate
By writing it down on paper.

Peering Into the Looking Glass

to women and balance within

As I peered into the looking glass
I saw my mother step at the edge
She slipped, fell through the illusionary ledge;
Free falling was exhilarating for her to experience
Be still, she shares dozens of reasons

In that moment she connected with my soul
It's as if she pulled me into her whole
I could dance with her through her life
Gleaning her golden nuggets so I could thrive

The greatest gift is immense love
I prosper as I pass it on as a dove
Only those who love themselves know
I feel telepathically even if they don't show

Transgender Niece

to women and balance within

The biggest change he went through
Was from seeing the world as an observer
To feeling everything in his/her heart.
Now she is no longer a searcher.

She now knows instead the joy of the female expression

FEELS other women's love without exception
(Men are busy with the outside world)
Switching one's basic thinking process is extremely bold

The delicate touch means so much to her beingness
Gentle strokes given and received are a magical plus
A drawback, however, is the awful pain of rejection
That deep connection with a woman
Then avoidance of her as if she has an infection

Her new sense of hope is like a bouncing ball
Her heart is lifted by the possibilities of a call
And why not be open for a stranger with compassion
Who harbors a mutual dream of a companion?

Giving up past alliances
She creates first on paper her most desired sequences,
Embracing her vision most voluptuous,
Peering into the probability of a new kind of play and wonder!

Bipul Banerjee is a sales and marketing professional with an MBA, currently pursuing a PhD in marketing. He writes poetry for the passion of expression, inspired by the emotions he comes across in day-to-day life. He has three research publications to his name and aspires to publish his own poetry collection.

Maturity

Cracking open the stone heart of mountains,
Gurgling with youthful force,
Young,
Virgin,
Crystal clear,
The waterfall of life
Gushes past all odds,
Taking along boulders, stones, rocks of resistance
Washing away all inhibitory inertia

The music,
The floor,
A loud different genre
Creating paths,
Dancing through,
Making a bed
Now called river
Steady yet powerful
Deep yet serene,
Helping the oars of life
To carry on
Anchoring the tired
Resting the boats
Talking to sails
Helped by occasional winds
To move on.

Meditating on the banks

Are the same crystal waters
Knowing the gush has ebbed,
Flowing strongly yet untiringly
Journeying towards the ultimate
Sea of Love…a destination that encompasses
The very being
Into ultimate sublimity of divine.
No whirl created by a pebble throw
Is capable of such distraction—
Immortal Dusk waits to witness this maturity
Which the river has brought along.

Dance in the Rains

Kick the puddles on the way.

Stain your clothes

Play with clay

Build castles of sandy hope on sea sides of emotions

Let them stand fearless against the crushing waves

A beautiful flower,

A stretch of green,

An outstretched toy,

A train of joy.

Find Joy in little things.

Break the mould of post-adolescent furnaces

Bring life back to the child within…

Happy,

Carefree,

Selfless and Honest.

Bring out these words from the closets of books.

Give them to the inner child

A piece of paper,

A kite of happiness,

A soft toy,

A cradle of busyness,

The flying butterfly,

The busy pup,

The summation of unlimited pleasure

Which the adult seeks and only the child can truly enjoy.

Dr. Mike is the pen name of Dr. Michael Harold Davis, PhD, a medical and environmental researcher of Scotch-Irish, Welsh, and German heritage. Growing up in the Seattle area, he later earned BS and PhD degrees in biochemistry. He has taught biochemistry at the college level, and is currently working on a book about epigenetics—the science of how environment affects genes.

Helen R. Davis (Ed)

We Can Never Be Happy Again
dedicated to all my ancestors and my daughter

Oh, we are the Welsh, Scotch, and Irish
The peoples who lost to the English then
Conquered the world as the British,
But, we can never be happy again!

Oh, it was a long time ago and as the British
We did thrive and grow but 'tis better
To down our bitters, Scotch, whiskey and whine
We can never be happy again!

Oh, the world now acclaims all thing Irish,
The whiskey, the songs, and the dance,
But that was because we were British,
And can never be happy again!

None of us really speak Welsh, Scotch or Gaelic,
But our American and European friends say,
"Is what you're speaking really English?"
And we can never be happy again.

We migrated 'round the world and
Colonized every place that we could.
Our descendants may have settled two continents,
But we'll never be happy again.

To those of the leftist academe,
Who live their lives on a screen

Our descendants are portrayed like Conan the Barbarian,
So we can never be happy again.

Ingratitude rules modernity
And people mistake viral for true,
Whatever it is that they're hearing,
It's not the truth of our ancestors
Which is why no will ever be happy again.

Helen R. Davis (Ed)

Doc Krinberg is a multi-award-winning poet and California native who has in his lifetime been a deep sea diver, strip club barker, junk yard truck driver and taxi driver. He's lived in Hawaii, Asia and the "mainland," and when desperate finally did a doctorate degree in education.

Poetry publications include FIFTY-EIGHT STONES: 2012 Savant Anthology of Poetry; BELLWETHER MESSAGES: 2013 Savant Poetry Anthology; THE BLACK ROSE OF WINTER (Lost Tower Publications, 2014); RUNNING FROM THE PACK: 2015/16 Savant Poetry Anthology; and TEMPTATIONS (Lost Tower Publications, 2016).

Prose publications include POLONIO PASS (Aignos 2014); THE DEEP SLUMBER OF DOGS (Aignos, 2016).

Clarity

The distance meant nothing
The pull
As intense as a moon
Locked in Jupiter's sway
I circled you
Your words swirling
Like dust devils
On the empty landscape
That was me
They spoke to me
The pull
I loved you deeply
I circled you
The wrong orbit
The wrong time
The wrong love

And so I stopped.

The Girl in Shinjuku Station

She rolled her skirt top

It pulled higher thighs exposed

Long stockings stark white
Men in the station

Below her on the stairway
Each in their own thoughts
Private images

Shame extinguished them quietly
Her silent lovers

North Shore Return

to the honey-girl of Makakilo

Time stops; Gatsby's clock.
Kisses from full lips pushing me
back to a year in Hale'iwa

Breathing the scent of her hair,
soft and curling in between
younger, worshipful fingers

Her plumeria settled, embedded.
Subtle white, yellow hues against skin,

sweetly, open and ready but piquant

This kiss igniting my senses
pushing, fleeing to those years before,
gray drains away, lost on the tides

Jock Armour, an art gallery director in Honolulu, spent his early years in Las Vegas, Scotland, and Ohio. He spends most of his time with his muse—the ocean.

Ode to the Cereus
for J.

Oh how the ridge does come alive

Beneath the mid-day blaze

And fragrant blossoms gently sway

Above the floral stage

The Orchid grows with slender ease

As she drinks the summer rays

Flaunting colors for all to see

Is how she spends her days

Hibiscus has a noble cause

For soaking up the glare

To signify a fellows love

Behind his lady's ear

But hidden underneath it all

Amidst the shades of green

Lies the suns one true love…

The Honolulu queen

With quiet grace she sips the light

The other flowers abhor

Her modest nature stirs delight

The sun, he does adore

He burns and burns, each ray for her

While others seem to plunder

She yearns and yearns, yet hesitates
He soon begins to wonder
The rest, you see, translate his love
In bright exaggerations
But only Cereus, in modest grace
Knows anticipation
"Please, my queen, take your share—
You have not but a thorn"
And to the sun she only smiles
Her love for him is torn
What tragic fates of time and love
Could keep her from his light?
A secret that she dare not share—
She only blooms at night
The Roses and the Lili koi
Try to gain affection
But the sun no longer sees their color
Nor looks in their direction
The days they pass, the sun he waits
High up in the sky
Until one day his heart does break
And slowly starts to cry
"Why, my love, oh why can't you—
Just open up your heart?"
And to his tears she says but this;

"We're half a world apart"
For when the day upon the ridge
Surrenders final light
There lives a world beneath the stars—
A still and quiet night
In all his youth, his brazen glow
He felt that he was king
But by his sight, through vanity
He could not see a thing
And still he burns, just like before
Upon the floral stage
But tempered by his newfound plight
His light he now does gauge
The Plumeria and the Morning Glory
Thirst for more and more
And yet he rations all his might
To visit his amore
The fates of time and circumstance
Has broken many a-will
But by the moon he steals a glance
Upon the quiet still
And there she reigns, as others sleep
Tired from the day
His bonnie queen does see him peek
And whispers "come what may"

From months of patient nourishment
She gathers up her plume
The time it comes but once a year
Her heart begins to bloom
A sight which must be earned through time
He see's was worth the pain
Her ivory petals delight the stars
As view begins to wane
The sun he stares from worlds away
A truth he understands;
It was not he that gave to her—
But she, his growth demands
For love, you see, like time and light
Can travel near and far
His heart can burn throughout the night
And reach her as a star

Helen R. Davis (Ed)

Mr. Ben, as he is fondly called, is an internationally recognized author, poet, playwright, novelist, essayist, speaker and voice-over artiste, whose labor of love for humanity has inspired him to thirst for knowledge towards human advancement. Based in Lagos, Nigeria, Mr. Ben delights in reading, writing, meeting and communicating with people. His published works include SAVED BY HIS GRACE (Revival Waves of Glory 2017), MAYA INITIATE 39 (Revival Waves of Glory 2016), A SUCCESSFUL MARRIAGE (Revival Waves of Glory 2016), GOD'S LOVE FOR THIS PEOPLE (Revival Waves of Glory 2016), THE BROKEN MIRROR (Revival Waves of Glory 2016), THE CHRISTIAN MATRIX (Revival Waves of Glory 2016), 7 MISTAKES CHRISTIANS MAKE AND THE BENEDICTION (Revival Waves of Glory 2016), JOURNEY TO LOVE (Novum Pro 2016), CHRISTMAS TIME! (Novum Pro 2016), ONE MAN'S DEEP WORDS (United P.C. 2016).

Poured Out Thoughts:
My Thoughts
Heralding God's Magnificence

Lord, thank you for grace

For you are with me always as I run my race

Inspite of my nakedness, you shield me with your lace

By faith, I can move mountains

For you've made me an ace

Christ is my base

I can't be shaken by life's rays

For in God's presence, I'm more than all mays

And in Christ, I put my enemies at infinite bays

The Lord God is in charge of my case

For His word is greater than what anybody says

His death on the cross is greater than all my big pays

So, I've chosen to serve Him, Grace!

Poured Out Thoughts:
My Thoughts
Family

I am the symbol of unity

I am the showcase of magnanimity

I am the reason for marriage

I am not regarding age

I am the room where my members rage

(Yet) I am the reason for the home

I am the husband's and wife's foam

I am the reason man and wife stay warm

I am the inspiration behind children

I am the very society's pen

I am "Love Reign Supreme"

I ensure all members are at their prime

I put the very needed effects in the home on time

"Who are you?" asks Mr. Rhyme.

I simply reply: I am Family.

Poured Out Thoughts:

My Thoughts

Nature's Blessings

The sun's unparalleled beauty of illumination at day…

The moon's complementary brightness at night…

The earth's peculiarity of revolution…

The water's outstanding universality…

The wind's timeless motion…
The Fire's power of flaming warmth…
The plant's unique culture of adaptability…
The animal's lifestyle of survivability…
The loving relationship among all planets…
The monitoring positions of the stars…
The accommodating stance of the skies…
The Reality of humanity's consciousness…
Sum up to Nature's Blessings.

Poured Out Thoughts:
My Thoughts
Save Humanity

Save Humanity (aka Save Mankind)
Man seeks a savior
He goes about it using it vigor
He is aware of the rigor

Man looks at the environment
He figures the movement
He ensures it will last all moments

But:
Man discovers he's wrong
He thinks of the way out through his song
He works out his strong

Man searches for riches
He goes all out for the fishes
He thinks that they will meet his very wishes

But:
Man is dissatisfied
He is worried he is not gratified
He believes his agenda will be clarified.

Man goes after wellness
He seeks to work its happiness
He feels that's his essence

But:
Man realizes he's in a vicious circle
He devises the way-out of the ridicule
He's certain his IQ would bring the driving vehicle

Man seeks a life companion
He searches in passion

He's sure this won't take him to oblivion

But:
Man is failing over a time-a hundredth
He sees himself being swallowed up by the earth
He makes his priority death

This time…
Man seeks his kind
He engages with a tough find
He succeeds on the note: "Save Mankind"

Poured Out Thoughts:
My Thoughts
Dad Loves Me

Dad loves me
because He made me
Dad makes me trust him
because he made my team
Dad makes me strong
because he made me not want
Dad makes me smile

because he took care of my file
Dad makes me sleep well
because he made me well
Dad makes me work
because he made me walk
Dad makes me obey
because he kept 'Bad' at bay
Dad makes me pass life's test
because he made me life's best
Dad makes me read my book
because he made me the nook
Dad makes me a way
because he made me pray
Dad makes me alive
because he gave me a life
Dad makes me like everyone
because he made love anyone
Dad makes me preach
because he made me teach
Dad makes me modest
because he made me honest
Dad makes me eat
because he made me fit
Daddy loves me always! That's why I love him too!

Helen R. Davis (Ed)

Emily Anderson is a junior in the creative writing program at Marshall University, Huntington, West Virginia. She was born and raised in Miami, Florida, and moved to Ohio when she was 13. She is currently in the process of writing her first novel.

TO C-JAY

to my ever supportive boyfriend

my love is not a new love it has evolved over millennia;
        i cannot say anything new about the feeling in my gut i
have no revolutionary thoughts about
        the afterlife i cannot tell you how to fix a pulled thread-

my love is not a new love it has fermented in the rotting grapes
it has fermented in the rotting grapes.
i have fermented in the rotting grapes.
it has germinated in the redwoods and i have died and been re-
born.

i have endured frostbite and sunburns and stretched skin and
scars from hot water
i have cracked but never crumbled
so i must be stronger than mountains.

you must be stronger than mountains.

my life has waxed and waned
i have watched the dirt rain down and shield me from the hor-
ror

i have been bathed in light cast from fluorescent bulbs and
kerosene lamps and i have been baptized in
      the sun-
        i have watched black clouds collide and carve into the
earth
      like children with sticks in sand.

we have held seashells to our ears and listened closely.
we heard war
      or were those waves crashing?

Helen R. Davis (Ed)

Marianne Smith is an accomplished poet and an amazing aunt. Her poems has previously been published in RUN-NING FROM THE PACK (Savant 2015/16).

Helen R. Davis (Ed)

Love Will Find A Way

Inspiration: *Artist: Vanessa Mae*
         CD: The Violin Player
         Track 5-"Warm Air"

Hear our voice and hear our prayer
we've lost our way and don't seem to care
where we sleep tonight
teach us and guide us to the path
that shows the way to take us home
for we have lost our way

A baby cries alone at night
his mother not there for him again,
its just not right
alone he will go hungry and he may die
without a whimper so sadly
Show us the way home

Ohhhhhhhhhhhhhh

W've forgotten how to live
we've forgotten how to reach out to one another
forgotten how to give,
seem to forgotten how to hear
the sounds of our own voice
teach us how to care for one another

Hear our voice and hear our prayers
guide us to new ways to share
leads us, guide us safely home tonight
so we can sleep peacefully assured
love will find the way

Ohhhhhhhhh

Sister, brother, parents
cousins, friends and neighbors
each so fearful no one trusts the other
those we fear are torn asunder

Teach us how live and how to pray
how to work together (love will find a way)
teach us how to to cope (love will find a way)
with the challenges we face each new day
side by side
I know love will find the way

Helen R. Davis (Ed)

Carolina Casas, besides writing, has an interest in drawing and painting. A big fan of science fiction and fantasy, she find most of her inspiration for her writings from these two.

Dark Existence

When I was young,
there used to be something inside of me
That wanted to break free.
As I got older that thing became corrupted
Until one day I let it wither and die.
I watched as it was blackened
By my desires to hurt those who had hurt me,
Make them see what I saw every day
What they called justice, I called abuse
It plead out for me to help
Stretching its thin, rotting arms like a helpless baby
And like the merciless creature I've become,
I shied away from it.
The following day I went to work,
I didn't complain, nor I cried.
I stood still as the customers yelled at me
The dead souls of old women
Sucking on the blood of others
Living off their pity and money
Smirked as I just stood there
Uncaring, smiling, ready to do their bidding
And like they've seeing the sun
For the very first time

Those dark creatures backed away
And as the day went on,
I let myself fall
Deeper and deeper
Into the abyss they created for me
Until there was nothing left
Just another empty shell
Another dastardly being
Who walks among you
Who walks with you
Whom others no longer taunt
Nor befriend
Not dead, not alive
I live, I breathe
But I never feel
I just exist, I just do.

Imagined Lives

Suspended reality
When I looked at the mirror,
I imagined myself a Princess, a Queen, an artist,

Anything but what my reflection shows me
Somehow the wondrous worlds I conjured in my head
Seem more real than what awaits me every day
I get out of bed and see a stranger staring back at me
On the streets people pass me by
No greetings, nothing …
Except a blank expression as they stare unto their smartphones
We've become empty,
Soulless beings walking into the abyss
No purpose,
No conscience,
No sense of self
Question everything!
We are told
But what are we to question?
The food we eat?
The people we talk to on chat rooms?
Are we allowed to question?
Nod, look down -we're told
Obey!
When the real word is too insane for a sane mind
The sane mind creates its own reality
A reality of freedom,
A reality of choice.
A reality where I can be anyone or anything

Where merit equals triumph

Struggle, happiness

And thought is not a given.

But in the end, it is only that:

A fantasy.

A made up lie,

No more real than the box we are in.

Helen R. Davis (Ed)

Cigeng Zhang is a freelance English translator from Beijing, China. He began writing and posting English poems on an international website in early 2012. Poetry is a part of her.

Published poems include "Drunk Smile," in the Poetic Bond series III (Createspace 2013), "What Was Left" in IV (Createspace 2014), "Still for You/ At 8 O'clock/ The Moon, the Poet" in V (Createspace 2015), "Hey, Starling/ Special Reunion/ Wa Lan / One-line Tide" in VI (Createspace, 2016) as well as "Civet Cat" in PURRFECT POETRY (Lost Tower 2014), "Jungle Jewelry" in JOURNEYS ALONG THE SILK ROAD (Lost Tower 2015), "Blackie" in AND THE TAIL WAGGED ON (Createspace 2015) and "A Fist Is Not Everything" in SHOUT IT OUT (Createspace 2016).

Calla Lily

Snowy gauze floats down
the rivulet of heaven

The softest caress
dedicated to her skins

Feel the gentle touch
Fly past, the goldfinch

From head to toes
Who fondles her joyously?

She closes her eyes
Sets free a heart of lovesickness

Many a divine petal
Creeps into her soul…

"Calla Lily" was inspired by the famous painting of Diego Rivera for
the nude woman with calla lily. When my friend Gary introduced the
painting to me, I was attracted by the warm color and the natural
nude woman in the painting.

The Night of Love

Blazing dahlia wraps around his neck

He feels the surge of the amorous waves

Wildly flocking to his open chest

O! The Night of Love –

Please take out all of her for my love

I want it! I want it!

"The Night of Love" was dedicated to Frida Kahio, the wife of Rivera. When I saw her pictures, her beautiful nudity, charming looks and naturally feminine way shocked me. Also her incredibly hard experience impressed me a lot. She was my muse.

Who Do I Meet?

I hear the knocking

ti da ti da

Look outside the window

Why, no one appears

ti da ti da

Open the window

A kingfisher flying in
He jumps on my shoulder

Trying to show his shiny wings
He stretches his feathers

I take off my silk nightgown
Borrow his wings to dance

"Who Do I Meet", dedicated to my friend Dr Gary Krinberg who influenced me a lot on my poetry creation and art appreciation. My window always waits for such a vivid light from the different sky of the world.

Game

Cloud is my heart
Moon is your teardrop

You have no mood to watch me
I slip from the rim of the sky

Too late to wipe away your tears

Since you hide inside another cloud

"Game" was written for the poet like me. When I feel lonely, I always gaze at the moon chasing after it into another lonely sky.

Fish

a shoal of fish rush to you

day to day, hour to hour

you sit quietly on the shore

wait to fish a wonder

of a blue whirlpool

that belongs to you

"Fish" was written after I had seen the modern artistic painting of the same title by Rosemary Feit Covey, the good friend of Gary. Her great work hit my eyes like a rotational flow.

Helen R. Davis (Ed)

Thomas Koron was born in Grand Rapids, Michigan on May 19, 1977. He has attended Grand Rapids Community College, Aquinas College, Western Michigan University and the American Conservatory of Music. An award-winning poet, he remains active in Grand Rapids as a composer and performer. Thomas' works have appeared in BELLWETHER MESSAGES (Savant 2013) and RUNNING FROM THE PACK (Savant 2016).

Helen R. Davis (Ed)

Lament of the Banshee

She walks alone through the forest in white;
Under thick boughs she lets out her lament—
Holding her head and wailing in the night.

The wind is blowing so fiercely tonight—
Going places few others ever went,
She walks alone through the forest in white.

The moon in the sky shines so very bright,
And her entire journey has been spent
Holding her head and wailing in the night.

She sees the trees now veering to the right—
The path up ahead appears slightly bent;
She walks alone through the forest in white.

The night is dark, with no one else in sight—
To deliver a message, she's been sent
Holding her head and wailing in the night.

She sees the house, and steps up near the light,
With her bare feet touching the cold cement.
She walks alone through the forest in white,
Holding her head and wailing in the night.

Shining Eyes in the Dark

Beware of the shining eyes in the dark;
Dreaming by day, at night it never sleeps.
Its sharp claws dig in deep, leaving their mark
Upon every soft object while it creeps.
Walking down the hallway silent and slow;
Keeping its sight on the floor as it glides
Swiftly down the stairs, while watching below.
Behind a chair, it retires and hides;
On the prowl, it moves its head as it turns,
And thanks the fates for all nine of its lives.
It spots a rodent, and its hunger burns;
There's no escape from how quickly it dives.
   The mouse that had once roamed free is now gone,
   And the cat enjoys its feast until dawn.

Fireflies

They float dreamily through the summer night,
Across a soft, sky-lit sunset of red,
And their backs glow with a green colored light.

A fire in the woods is burning so bright,
Now that the true heat of the day has fled,

They float dreamily through the summer night.

From the trees in the forest they take flight,
Moving towards the shore of the lake instead,
And their backs glow with a green colored light.

Flying further now - intrigued by the sight
Of the cabin where their travels have led -
They float dreamily through the summer night.

A bright full moon gently bathes them in white,
As they fly past a window by the bed,
And their backs glow with a green colored light.

They circle through the air as we sleep tight,
Now dreaming of the cooler days ahead.
They float dreamily through the summer night,
And their backs glow with a green colored light.

On This Bed of Roses

On this bed of roses my teardrops fall,
As clouds begin to darken in the sky,
And vines have grown across the garden's wall.

A bird in the trees makes one final call—
I hear the wind let out a gentle sigh,
On this bed of roses my teardrops fall.

This storm is about to ravage them all—
The rain begins to drench me as I cry,
And vines have grown across the garden's wall.

Looking at the roses, I now recall
An innocent time forever gone by—
On this bed of roses my teardrops fall.

There once had been twenty rosebuds in all—
I wipe yet another tear from my eye,
And vines have grown across the garden's wall.

I once had dreams they'd grow so very tall,
But now, their pedals wither where they lie.
On this bed of roses my teardrops fall,
And vines have grown across the garden's wall.

Helen R. Davis (Ed)

Mark Daniel Seiler is a multi-award-winning writer and designer-builder who lives in Kalaheo. His debut novel, SIGHING WOMAN TEA (Xlibris 2014) was a winner at the Pacific Rim Book Festival 2015 and was nominated for the Kirkus Prize. Mark enjoys the similarities of designing a building with crafting a story.

www.sighingwomanteas.com

Helen R. Davis (Ed)

The Bare Tree State

The Buddhist held a green leaf hostage
demanding the immediate release of all concepts.
A hardliner drop of rain plunged to its death
protesting the radicalization of emptiness.
In solidarity, a cricket joined the moonlight
dancing on the top of my rain barrel.

Dwight Armbrust Jr is a 25-year-old poet, out of Charleston, South Carolina. He is a creative soul encouraged by his interactions with other true artists, lovers of life, and thrill seekers, believing that spirituality and balance are the keys to life and that all people share the same religion, Love.

One Love Can Not Count

to all who question going through pain to experience love

Amor like scores thrice, miniature stars, and foresights with smiles bright and pores tight, red carpet aisles, x-files and Latin textiles, informed life of a lover trapped in a body of melted butter, with a shell hot as hell patrolling kisses of cologne. Heavens stutter as your stroll replays in ways that condone insanity, in a heart where every beat exposes the scars of backwards starts in this love monopoly. Rest nonstop and see, me as my chest shows less autonomy to the botany of a flower that exhales less of love. Let my smile be Protection for the reservation of your heart. I love how you rip me apart. The thorns lavishly attack the flesh, but the pain is so lovely. A life without your affection is a realm of glorified death. Live forever and let die.

When will we know that the vanity of love cannot be tamed?

Poison Less Potions

to all who question going through pain to experience love.

Seductive exhales of ecstasy, golden barred hearts, pearls dripping from your aura. Her smile ignites my universe, exposing the orbital exchange of my being, perfection, almost. For me, perfect. Loyalty is her demeanor and she feeds on it as though her hunger boils. Tired of getting it wrong, we connect our rights, something special is all it can be deciphered as. A priceless releasing the energies that has jailed her love before we combined. Lovely concoctions could never explain reactions of interactions type black roses separating love from lust, as if Moses was the teacher, speakers pound as pain drowns his joy, simultaneously allowing mirrors of members to destroy themselves with prowess like redemption. Now nest within the wings of a teacher, concrete creatures exist, known to roll over clouds of ecstasy, Know no rains upon loveless lies despise everything we stand for.

Even GOD is love, so how we can escape the side effects of this potent level?

Candles as Organs
to all who question going through pain to experience love

Hearts infected by frostbite darken forever lit candles as mantles hold samples of what my smile used to be. Reborn into a world torn with remnants of love, the man above mentions better will come. An impossible love burns within me, questioning how simply can a smile so painfully ecstatic, stain my embrace of what sanity should be. Friendships forever written in the starry skies as lies never exist in this realm. Stars align as my mind blows as if mines were implanted in the minds of mines, what is a friend you might ask ? We can never have enough of them. But the ones that remain true are limited in a limitless vortex of falsified affection. Point me in the right direction to entertain a friendship with you. If impossible, remember there are other lifetimes.

Remember, melted hearts reform into eternal flames

Multi-award-winning poet, **Uhene (Robert Mai-ka'i Jr)**, lives in the beautiful, paradise state of Hawaii. Single, no children, he loves people and anything that tastes of the mango. His Grandfather, Kawika Smith from Molokai, took him to first theater movie at five years of age, a Samurai production, and thus began his poetic career on the streets of Waikiki.

Uhene's poems appear in BELLWETHER MESSAGES (Savant 2013) and RUNNING FROM THE PACK (Savant 2015/16).

Helen R. Davis (Ed)

O' Be The Light In My Life To Shine Forth With My Hands

O' Be the light in my eyes.
Be the light upon my hands.
Oh Lord My Guide
Be the light in my hand.
Be the light in my mind.
Be the light to reflect,
Your Love, Oh Lord
My Guide
Be the light in my life.
Be the light to share,
to others about your love,
Oh My God
Be the light in my hands.
Be the light in my mind.
Be the light to reflect,
Your Love Oh Lord,
My Guide

O2 Thomas

Despite my ignorance and rebellion,
He still desires to shine in and through me, He who made me
from dirt, yet He still desires to live in me!

He's first. When compared to this world, none can measure up.

In the valleys of the shadow and death, I have pitted myself in Him,

God desires me to live within the foundation He's laid to
build within me the heart of the better inner man. Oh! His gentleness and mercy loudly whispers forgiveness. As I continue to
walk on dirt, yet in His grace, I walk on gold, forever, with
Him, my Lord and God. The one and true living God, the one
and true living God who is like You, ABBA, Father. None
other!

You tell the sun to go asleep and awaken the moon to
shine so many will have a chance to still see you. Oh, God,
your tender mercy!

It is only You who is able to clothe Yourself with the
Heavens . If You so desire, it is for You to reveal Yourself.
None can comprehend You or Your clothing, even with the
light of the globe, my utmost imagination, my strongest desire.
None cannot comprehend how marvelous the love given .

Please help me, Abba, Father to carry my cross in Your truth . Teach me to listen, walk, abide and live in the happiness of the Holy Spirit . I do not want to be any longer a rebel, but a true child of the everlasting, in the lovely Name of Jesus, this I confess, pray and ask. Amen.

So Shook The Earth Nigh Of Night

It's all about the power of the blood , all its power.
How it finished for the Beloved on a hill called Calvary .
Do not cherish the torment of pain, or so much ravish the torment of shame, for the blood gives the power to shine as sparkling candlelight.
It's the blood that was shed that covers all debauchery cast upon ourselves. It's the power of the blood, as the cross is the open door to life evermore. Its the blood that, being shed on a tormented, demented cross, it the very power of life!

Be Cleansed By A Hand Of Love

Go being in God? In this, I have failed, oh, God, my Lord!

Restore me, please. Draw me out to be anew. Direct my mind
and heart to walk afresh in Your spirit of love, of love, of love..
Let me be cleansed, be cleansed, be cleansed.
Oh, live in the spirit of love!
Take my innermost parts; make them grow in Your grace, in
the presence of Your divine, beautiful love.
Let me be cleansed, be cleansed, be cleansed!
Help me to depend on you and reflect the beauty that is above !
Give me the assurance and the presence of Your love
To be cleansed, be cleansed, be cleansed!
Teach me how to rest assured of Your beauty within my heart ,
My life with your endless love, so endless a love!

Called to be What I Truly Could and Should Be

I'm called to be a vessel, to proclaim His name,
A name to acquaint others of his marvelous work.
I am like everyone else—of similar molecular, cellular makeup
So let's be real when I say I am just wanting to be led by the
Holy Spirit's name, that that's the only way I'm going to learn
to share hearts.

It happens when the HolySpirit jolts something within,
Leaving one aching to be touched, motivated, inspired.
To what? Share, "Preach unto all?"
No, not by thinking I know any answers with a lifted up nose,
But simply by shouting out my own need to be
Touched.
Motivated.
Inspired.
Because it's for the Holy Spirit and God to give and received
all the glory. Only one thing can penetrate the human shell, and
it is that all may remember how to know, say and think the
most proficient and deliberate thing: That is to gain conscience
and consider God in all His ways.
To thrive in whatever we do, means being a vessel blazes forth
Almighty God and *His* honor and glory.
So do bring me, oh, Lord, to your basin,
Your basin of love,
Where the pure living water pours out
And let me soak in it within Your presence forever,
To become so evermore grateful for your showering of bless-
ings unto me.
As Your heir, I want to steep in Your promise of being adopted
as Your Son, a child who lives without thirst or wants,
Completely fulfilled with Your beloved Son, Jesus .

Daniel S. Janik is a multi-award-winning poet, author, and movie producer. Visit with him at http://janik.yolasite.com. His published works include QUANTUM DEATH (Savant 2016), THE TURTLE DANCES (Savant 2013), A WHALE'S TALE (Savant 2009), SOURDOUGH SCOTT'S BEDTIME FAIRY TALES FROM ALASKA (Publication Consultants 2005), FOOTPRINTS, SMILES AND LITTLE WHITE LIES (Savant 2008), THE ILLUSTRATED MIDDLE EARTH, LAST AND FINAL HARVEST (Savant 2008), UNLOCK THE GENIUS WITHIN (Rowman & Littlefield Education, 2005), A NEUROBIOLOGICAL THEORY AND METHOD OF LAN-GUAGE ACQUISITION (Lincom Europa, 2004), HOW TO CHOOSE THE BEST ENGLISH LANGUAGE SCHOOL IN THE USA (Authorhouse, 2006). His poems appear in RUN-NING FROM THE PACK (Savant 2015/16), VOLUTIONS (Savant 2014), BELLWETHER MESSAGES (Savant 2013), FIFTY-EIGHT STONES (Savant 2012), WAVELENGTHS (Savant 2011), and FIRST BREATH (Savant 2010). He is the multi-award-winning producer of "Clean Water, Common Ground" (National Film Network, 1999)

Phantoms of the Night

My words are phantoms of the night,
They vibrate and twist about,
Like dull rain clouds
Beneath tavern gas lamps,
In search of holes in the mouldings.

Never have I known a midnight fog like this,
So dense that it soaks into bone
As fast as a word,
Nor blind the eyes and heart
Like a word.

Flames are lit on church candles,
On alters of midnight Easter chanting masses,
Yet all their light and radiance
Are but momentary barriers
To the ever growing darkness
Carried in the arms of my words.

Be warned!
There is no light so bright
Nor night so dark
That you or your love can crawl out from

Beneath the hovering phantoms of
My words.

New Walls

What beautiful walls these
That shelter me in the night.
Yet,
If a shelter from the cold outside,
Then also a barrier from any warmth
Outside
Wherein a God whose heart is said to know no bounds
Glides soundlessly this way and that
As if searching for a home.
Who knows?
Except the walls.
It is said to be a sacrilege
To pray inside
Standing upon a rug;
If only I could kneel
Upon a floor of dirt and mud,
I could then bow my head in anguish
And cry the long-held soul tears—

I have forgotten how to cry real tears—
And know my search at last, is over.

If I had my way…
If I had my way,
I would tear these walls down!
If I had my way…
If I had my way.
So, if Truth and Light do exist,
And there really is a narrow path leading
The way to them,
Then let me have my way!
Let me tear these walls,
These buildings, down!

Society protects,
While humankind builds little walls,
From the dirt I would be kneeling on
To protects us from…
What?
Truth? Light? Ourselves?

If I had my way
(humankind is blinded by society's spectacles)
If I had my way…

(humankind fears that which it cannot see or taste or hear or…)
If I had my way…
(beasts can crawl; humankind alone has lost this gift)
If I had my way…
(Even God swears by the American flag, isn't that so?)
If I had my way…
I would damn this callous world
And tear all the walls down.

But I don't.
I haven't.
At least, I think I haven't.
I have
Walls.

Another Poem Echo

This small world is mine: Let me be!

Somewhere in everyone's substance
There is a golden pea
Untouched by eyes,
inquisitive fingers,

wondering noses.
In all the world there is,
Perhaps,
But this which is one's own.

A toss of sunbleached blond,
Two lips,
two breasts,
A hidden star and wish.

All the world
A golden pea.

Decidedly Exogenous

If love does exist my love, my dear,
I say,
My dear,
Then it was born on your lips,
And cradled deep
In the vocal cords of your heart.

It was not a breath

But the breathless rhythm of your labored stare
That sensed what I heard you say
When I thought you said, "I love you."

Helen R. Davis (Ed)

Lonner F. Holden had his first poem published at the

age of seven. A contributor to the internationally awarded Savant 2014 Anthology "Volutions" he has also been published in the 2004 and 2005 Marin Poetry Center Anthologys. Lonner lives in California as a healing arts practitioner and nature connection mentor.

Helen R. Davis (Ed)

Midspan Hercules

The great red hammock of
the Golden Gate Bridge dangles
from the shadow of a lone raven.

Balancing on a tightrope of gusts,
obsidian shoulders notched squarely
into puffed cheeks of fog -
his feathery kite lifts as if his
cargo is no burden at all.

The steel span lounges in space,
tugs at the tether of the
tiny winged black god who

mocks this mortal triumph of
engineering and proportion
with merely an invisible
thread borrowed from the sun.

Wiser Trees

In long absent rains
the forest weeps:
old trees tears of relief

young trees tears of
naive mimicry too young
to yet understand

in drought roots must
entwine within ever
hardening ground as

wiser trees together
brace the forest against
an imprisoning Earth

the impermeable clay
offering nothing but
a great waiting.

Helen R. Davis (Ed)

Mother Moon

the moon serves
her cool milk

whispers a lullaby
in breezes that

rock the wild cradle
of oak branches

marsh rushes
poppy blossoms

eyes fast asleep
hold us close to

the bosom of night
with instinct we

can only feel
by our surrender

Pointillist

Driving by a wash of
Forget-me-nots along the road -
tiny bubbles, Spring champagne
uncorked, spill over foam popping

on my eyes fizz down nerve
trails to a boy lying next to his
mother bathed by open sky
in alpine wildflower spritz;

warmed by far north
fading Summer sun
high above the
shimmering fjord.

Bees buzz flower to flower
our fingers blueberry stained
laughter tossed carefree
into our sparkling bouquet;

her whole being smiling
illumined, weightless,
eyes star sapphires, lips

gently stitched to rosy cheeks,
errant amber hairs frolic
with tugging gusts.

She smiled at times like those,
and only those, peace
known by the wild
freedoms around her;

her smile the smile you
see in a person only when
they are happy,
true blue happy.

Opening the Door One Morning

In your sleep you did not know
the simple thank you came to
alight at your doorstep;
a benediction stirring
within a thin envelope.

You thought the

light from the morning sun
woke you…

But it was instead the return
of a white feather that had
once fallen from your heart onto
the life of a young woman
who needed to fly.

Helen R. Davis (Ed)

Sara Hawley grew up in Coventry, Ohio, and attended college at Casper College in Casper, WY. She was married, but is now divorced.

Her previous works include "To Ian" (not available online).

Helen R. Davis (Ed)

I Can't Live Without You

Being with you makes my spirit soar

My love for you

Is greater than any love I've ever known

I want to spend eternity in your arms

Your eyes show me the future

Your smile is the most amazing thing in the world

Your scent drives me crazy

I can't get enough of you

That's why I can't live without you

Born in Eastern Europe, Ihar Kazak lived in West Germany, East Africa, West Switzerland, and now resides in Central Florida. Formerly an interpreter, he traveled with U.S. technical and medical teams in the Soviet Union, then Russia and elsewhere. He is now a literary translator, translating the pioneering work of the humorist émigré writer Arkady Averchenko, as well as works by the renowned authors Vasyl Bykov and Leanid Levanovich. He has also rendered his father's collection of Belarusian poetry into English: "Love for the Homeland: A Collection of Belarusian Poetry" by Ryhor Krushyna (currently in search of a publisher).

He has his own unpublished collections of poems designed to introduce English readers to the proverbial Slavic soul, prone to sadness, nostalgia, humor and the entire gamut of human emotions. Other unpublished poetry collections include "Idiomatic-Idiotic-Idiosyncrasies," "On the Veranda of Life," and his most current collection, "Human Delusions," while many more poems wait impatiently in his head and heart.

Helen R. Davis (Ed)

The Ha-Ha Society:
A Modern Fable

Once upon a time someone quipped:
Laughter is healthy!
And so the public began to
Ha-ha, hee-haw, snicker,
Snort, giggle, guffaw,
Howl, cachinnate, cackle
And a dozen other variants.
Passing women, upon the first encounter,
Smiled readily.
Wall Street folks grinned and chuckled.
TV news folks cracked jokes,
But offered little news.

TV comedies offered canned laughter.
Soon enough no one was serious,
For everyone wanted to be healthy.
Frivolity was reverberating in the land.
Laughter prevailed at all social levels.
Even the President started joking around.
Salespeople, officials, and even conmen
(conwomen and congays, as well),
Would smile and say: "Have a good laugh!"

No one took life seriously,
They began to take lives
Left and right,
And mostly abroad
By brute force and bombing.

But everyone thought
That they were so-o healthy.
They even laughed
(especially one Party)
At statistics:
Almost half of the population
Had no health insurance.
Why need it since
We're so-o healthy?
They even laughed off
Their infant mortality rate,
Which was second in the Developed World.
They laughed so hard their
Flabby-pudgy bodies shook in mirth.

After all, they were leading
The World in obesity.
And so the public,
Willy-nilly laughed over

The insipid TV/movies
Dished out to them.
Folks who had ample time
On their hands
Since they could not engage them
Being unemployed and idle.
So they laughed off their
Jobless fate,
Whilst a smaller percentage
Laughed all the way to the bank.

The Ha-ha Society is still laughing,
Pooh-poohing climate change.
Grinning in self-satisfaction
For being the most
Democratic,
Most
Heavily armed,
Most
Influential.
Most ridiculed and
The most *mostest* nation
Of the rest of the world.
And so its people laugh for health,
Never mind the wealth and stealth.

One elusive, the other intrusive.
Ha-ha! let's laugh it off, it's healthy.

The story teller has duly observed his milieu.

Checks and Balances

When we were kids in school
we were told in civics class
about our Great Democracy
so wisely based on
checks and balances.
With age and despite its
strange regress
it has become perfectly clear to us that
indeed, there are
checks and balances
in our system.
Fat-cats in corporations get their
multi-million dollar checks
while Joe and Jane try desperately
to balance
their meager accounts.
Remembering that civics class
it now becomes axiomatic that

our democracy is indeed
so wisely based on
checks and balances.

Morose thoughts on the equilibrium in a democracy and the edacious
greed of gain and usual usury.

Barbara Bailey is a word and clay artist.

Helen R. Davis (Ed)

Ballet of the Undulates

The rooster sounding greetings, to a new bright morning
Songs sung by the little brown hen

Answering new beginnings

All in sound to the rhythm

Piglets dancing a minuet
Bowing to their partners

Grace and elegance displayed

Moving to the rhythms

Not to be outdone, cows balance on their toes
Spinning a pirouette

In the shadow of their silhouette

Stepping to their rhythms

Reaching for the sky
Goats, a twisting leap

The higher they insist

Ballet rhythms of the barnyard

Would, Could, Should

Would I if I could
Would I if I should
Would I if I would

Should I if I could
Should I if I should
Should I if I would

Could I if I could
Could I if I should
Could I if I would

Maybe none of the above

Autumn's Song

Sheep in the dark valley
Down from the golden hills
Stirring under barren trees
Through rustling of the mills

Gentle to their rest they go
Sipping from the stream
Evening brings its dewy breath
Touching every dream

Crystals ice and wait to dance
In morning's misty light
Sheep come come – sheep come come
Meadow's autumn light

Burn Out

The heart longs for flame
two becoming one

in the essence of each moment
loving and loving not

The flash, the fire, the flame
embers fading

to ash and art
loving and loving not

Fed with thought
consumed with mind

desire feeling and feeding again
loving and loving not

Helen R. Davis (Ed)

V. Bright Saigal is an India-born American writer, poet, novelist, screen writer and film Director. He is currently working as a Marketing, Communication and Creative-Consultant while fundraising for Hollywood film projects. He is an alumnus of the Indian Institute of Mass Communication. In the USA, Barbara Watkins an America novelist and Dr. Zachary Oliver, an author and poet, who encouraged him to contribute to FIRST BREATH (Savant 2010). His other published works include THE PHILOSOPHY OF GOVERNANCE (Lulu 2011), AAA-POEM BOOKS-LULLABY (A COLLECTION POEMS & STORIES BY V. BRIGHT SAIGAL) (International Voice Tribune, 2011), and the IVT WORLD QUIZ MASTER series (IVT, multiple dates).

His debut novel LONDON MARSHALL will soon be released.

Helen R. Davis (Ed)

Jingles of Laughter

Crowning those memories, Once clouded under the sorrow
Yet again arising like the sun in the horizon
Lit in my heart a ray of hope where unending darkness pre-
vailed once
The broken strings at the bosom, vibrating profound once again
Resonating those jingles of your laughter
Flying up the lost memories from
Under the ashes of the bad days once clouded me
Like butterflies flying up from the blossoming garden in the
spring, at last
Filling the memories of mine in seven color
Once prevailed in my heart like a rainbow
Budding those tender feelings lapping my heart like ripples
Once again arriving the constellation of winking stars
Turing my life a festive of happiness
Every wing is coming echoing your laughter
Echoing a rhythm ruled my heart once
From every notes of lute and love

Percussion of Waves

The percussion of wild waves slows down at last
Arising hopes and filling happiness brushing a million hues
Animated butterflies hopping across the garden
Awaiting for the moments once and ever
Longing for your laughter, waking up the string of love at the
abyss
The brook in my heart waking up,
Laughing at me like teasing my sorrows
Paving way for the new dawn of the spring
Clamor of happiness heard beneath somewhere
The celebration of started at at once again
Forgotten days were buried under the ashes of memories
I lived for long years, pampering swelling heart
Healing those wound, once bled for long time
Pampering of your memories smoothened deep wounds
Arriving the ender breeze coddle s me again
Has the spring decided to stay longer?
Lied in my heart you A perennial brook,
Still live the way your tender adoration and love
I longed for ever, live in my like an oasis
Let my life blossom once again, and again.

Helen R. Davis (Ed)

Ken Rasti, also known as "Yes" among friends, is a professor at several universities and a business management consultant for multiple organizations. He recently was inducted into the Heroes of Humanity Hall of Fame in recognition of his positive community contributions with Aloha at the center of his heart. An award-winning-poet, his poem "Aloha, I Love You: We are All Connected" appeared in BELLWETHER MESSAGES - 2013 Savant Poetry Anthology. He has had a prose article of the same name published in a book entitled MESSAGES OF PEACE (Inspired Wellness, 2013). He lives in Hawaii, and has a daughter and a son in California.

Helen R. Davis (Ed)

Deeper than the Sea

to my son Dimitri

Rest in the arms of love
In the joy and beauty of being you

Be calm
Be true
Let love watch over you

Climb the steep hills of your life's journey
And what do you see?
The view, the grandeur, the progress,
Or the tiredness in your stumbling feet?

Let your vision be deeper than the sea
Search for the hidden treasures
In the everlasting arms of hope
Trust
They will be found

And they will be deeper than the sea

Sailing

to my daughter Mitrah

I was sailing away
Sometimes against the wind
I was riding on the subway
Sometimes making many stops

The earth gave way
The mountains fell into the heart of the sea
It all made my unruly mind wonder

I waited, eyes in twilight
For the promise that
Everything will turn out right
Right or wrong
Was I deceiving myself?

I was floating on a dream
On the magic

I heard love whisper to me
To marvel the beautiful
Surrender my ways completely to love

I wondered, could it be…
Love's will, not mine
Love's strength, not mine
Love's gifts, eternal light…

Love whispered to me
To listen to the voice in my heart
Saying, you'll know what to do
Let me lead the way
On the subway of life

Sweet Moon

to my precious mom, Minoo

There's a full moon rising slowly tonight
There's a heart of gold beating softly tonight
Come a little bit closer, hold your breath softly
I want to dance with you, my sweet moon
Life is a dance floor
I came into existence on that floor
On a night like this
When a full moon was slowly rising
That sweet moon dwells in me, as me
She makes me believe in love again

I celebrate her radiant song
The Blue Bird is singing to her
I ask her to come and sit by my side
Smile in silence
Smile in mind
Smile in heart
Smile is a medicine women

When my sweet moon smiles
She illuminates my way home
I open the window and invite her in
Her light, clear and close, the only companion of my soul

When the North wind blows
When my home feels dark, she always keeps me warm
So softly, until dawn

I whisper, let me get lost in your love
She smiles

There's a full moon slowly rising tonight
Come a little closer
Dance with me

Helen R. Davis (Ed)

Nature's Ecstasy

to my precious mom, Minoo

Prepare a feast by the lakeside
Surprise
The joy of the spring
The song of a sweet sparrow

Revel in Mother Nature's joy
Her every moment is a part of eternity

Mother Nature has been weary
Yet even after long months of winter
She is the embodied spirit of beauty in the world

Treat her softly as a messenger of love
A saint with a mission to heal

Sense the presence of her Spirit in a spring flower
And live a life of childlike wonder

Nature's Ecstasy

Mother Nature knows Your Nature
Even when you swim upstream against

The current of her purpose
Let her Spirit guide you through treacherous waters

Breathe deeply
Share your love with Mother Nature

Prepare a feast by the lakeside

Dolphins

to my daughter Mitrah

A secret place of being
Where the soul is calm
Where all is real

I feel their pain
Let me make it disappear into
The presence of love

Let the dolphins dance
Come
Let us dance with them

Invite passion and joy to join in the dance
Let fantasy whisper softly

And attitude
Let each moment be a choice to practice the
Presence of love or
If you must, the
Presence of fear

Freedom
I find in my joy when I follow my heart
My breath

Victim
I find a prison in me when I follow my head
My thoughts

Learning is enlightening
But unlearning is liberating

Trust
Love shall bring it all to pass
Shine
It's never too late to be childlike
Swim
Your ultimate destination is safe and secure
Swim with the dolphins
Swim with the mystics

Teuta S. Rizaj was a professor and educator for many years. She is the author of THE SLICED LAND AND OTHER STORIES (Createspace 2015) and THE RHAPSODY OF THE ANT WOMAN: POEM WITH COMPLEMENTARY DRAW-INGS (Createspace 2014). Her award-winning poems have appeared in newspapers and magazines, as well as in RUNNING FROM THE PACK (Savant 2016). She has translated and authored nonfiction books, book reviews, articles, and studies. Apart from writing, she enjoys drawing, painting, and the company of seekers of truth.

Helen R. Davis (Ed)

What of Truth?

The subtle lies can weave thick mists
Even over the Greatest Truths;
To those the Greatest Gift was given,
Under their rugs, they hide it—
They step on it, spit on it, and deny it;
In their thoughts like ice, they freeze it,
And in their actions like iron, they kill it.

Their shallow pretence stirs
All the clamor of tongues at once:
"What of Truth? We know not of such Gift!
Give us greed and power fitly mated—
In lying, in stealing, in killing to coexist."

While still in a deep rotting sleep
And the earth shakes under their feet,
The tricksters and tyrants and charlatans
Smitten on the head with the coldness of death
Awaken among the agonies of their calamities.

"Bring in the graveman or the ploughman,"
They urge, in the straits of distress:
To uncover the Truth and dig out the Gift—

From the raw fleshes of unserious hearts,
Stained with blood, the stinking clot.

But What of Love?

"But what of Love?" the Builder asked.
Love grows slowly like the forest tree—
From the inner heart toward the outside.

Let's build then a house of humanity:
Equality its foundation,
And Liberty its roof.

Equality pours the Light on each pillar,
Like the sunrays in their peak,
Which Each makes to All.

Liberty is the common birth-right
As is the common grave—
So make the house blossom into Life,
And build, not destroy, in Love's name.

Helen R. Davis (Ed)

A Moment of Silence

A moment of silence, that's all we need—
To shun unbounded vain conversations,
And take a thought like a frog a leap
Into the intentions of the One-Page Book,
Wherein nothing has been neglected.

All the like visitations: calamities, tribulations;
The swelling, the shrinking, the burning of
Fiery elements that seize us in open or unawares,
Holding each meddling hand accountable—
All so well-intended to make us grow humble.

With fellow ants we may seek a way down
Into the earth, but not a ladder up unto the sky.
So the grueling change of creation we must taste—
Those shriveling sacks in the twister's dance,
While feel helpless but still ablaze
With wanton, decadent celebrations.

The Truest Joy is a Serious Concern
(Res Severa Verum Gaudium)

Your persistence kept me in this world
But this New World will be empty
If you're not in it. —
The moon will turn warm,
The sun will turn cold;
There'll be no place to rest,
And no place to live.

Look, how face without joy turns pale
Like the lone sorrowful moon;
How cheeks become hollow
Like ancient obscured caverns.
But if the truest joy sweeps but once,
Red roses on the hollow cheeks would bloom.
Who says then this New World awaits its doom?